ORIGAMI SAFARI

STEVE AND MEGUMI BIDDLE

Illustrated by Megumi Biddle

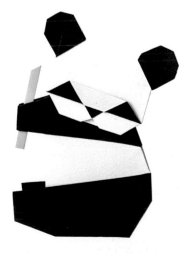

RED FOX

ABOUT THE AUTHORS

Steve Biddle is a professional entertainer with a speciality act that has taken him all over the world. He studied origami in Japan with the top Japanese origami masters, thereby acquiring deeper knowledge of a subject that has always fascinated him. Megumi is a highly qualified graphic artist, designer and illustrator, with a long-standing interest in paper and its many applications.

Steve and Megumi combine their talents to design items for television, feature films and major advertising campaigns, and in writing books for children and adults.

They have taken their craft all over the country to schools, festivals and arts centres and currently present a weekly origami programme for Sky TV.

A Red Fox Book

Published by Random House Children's Books
20 Vauxhall Bridge Road, London SW1V 2SA

A division of Random House UK Ltd
London Melbourne Sydney Auckland
Johannesburg and agencies throughout the world

First published in 1994 by Red Fox

Text © Steve and Megumi Biddle 1994
Illustrations © Megumi Biddle 1994

Set in Garamond
Printed and bound in China

RANDOM HOUSE UK Limited Reg. No. 954009

ISBN 0 09 922741 X

INTRODUCTION

Make a world of animals in paper! Using simple paper-folding know-how, Origami Safari takes you on a journey around the world, from the Northern Polar regions, to the Australian outback and other exciting places in between. Learn how to make elephants, tigers, monkeys and many other amazing creatures.

When making displays of origami it is the finishing touches and your own personal style that will make your scenes look professional. By all means, aim to copy the arrangements as they appear in the photographs at first, but what is important is how you develop the illustrated ideas. All that you need to create a lifelike scene is: a few pieces of craft card, scissors, glue and a little imagination.

You may be wondering what sort of paper to use for the origami projects. All of the models in this book are folded from a square of paper, although in many cases you'll need more than just one. All kinds of paper can be folded into origami, but do try to find paper that suits you best. Packets of origami paper, coloured on one side and white on the other, can be obtained from department stores, toy shops, stationery shops and oriental gift shops, other suitable paper can be found in art and craft shops. Why not try using the fancy gift wrapping papers that are now widely available? You could even cut out a few pages from a colour magazine!

To help you become accomplished at paper folding, here are some very helpful tips:

• Try to take great care in obtaining the right kind of paper to match the origami that you plan to fold. This will help enhance the finished product.

• Before you start, make sure your paper is square.

• Fold on a flat surface, such as a table or a book.

• Make your folds and cuts neat and accurate.

• Press your folds into place by running your thumb nail along them.

• Remember that in the illustrations, the shading represents the coloured side of the paper.

• Above all, if a fold or a whole model does not work out, do not give up hope. Put the fold to one side and come back to it another day.

If you want to learn more about origami, contact the British Origami Society, 11 Yarningale Road, Kings Heath, Birmingham, B14 6LT.

In the United States, contact the Friends of the Origami Center of America, 15 West 77th Street, New York, NY 10024-5192.

We would very much like to hear from you about your interest in origami, or if you have any problems obtaining origami materials. So please do write to us, care of our publishers, enclosing a stamped addressed envelope.

We hope you have a great deal of fun and enjoyment with Origami Safari. Happy folding!

Steve and Megumi

CONTENTS

PENGUIN

Habitat

shores of Antarctica and on islands off Australia, New Zealand, South Africa and southern South America.

Origami folds look most effective when displayed together. So why not try making a display of penguins?

You will need:

Square of paper, black on one side and white on the other

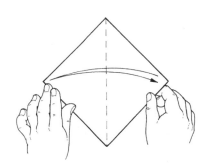

1 Turn the square around to look like a diamond, with the white side on top. Fold and unfold it in half from side to side.

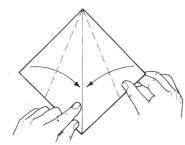

2 From the top point, fold the sloping sides in to meet the middle fold-line, so making a shape that in origami is called the kite base.

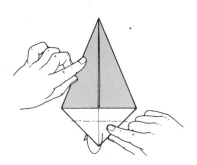

3 Fold the bottom point behind.

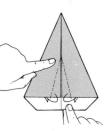

4 Fold the middle flaps of paper behind as shown.

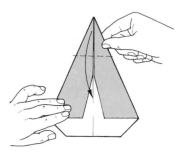

5 Fold the top point down, so making the penguin's head.

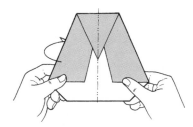

6 Fold the left-hand side behind to the right-hand side.

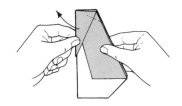

7 Holding the penguin as shown, pull its head upwards, so it becomes free and sticks out from the folded side.

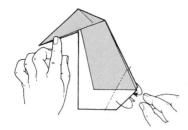

8 Press the top of the penguin's head flat. Fold the bottom right-hand point up inside the model. Repeat behind.

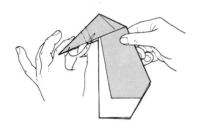

9 Now double inside reverse fold the penguin's head. This is what you do, ...

10 push the head down inside itself as shown.

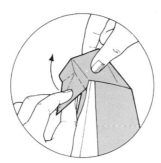

11 Pull the head up as shown. Press the paper flat, so ...

12 making the penguin's beak.

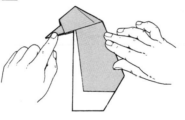

13 Here is the completed penguin.

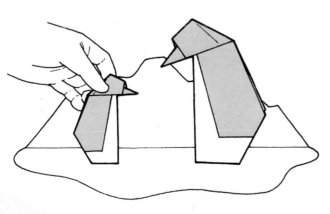

14 As with all of the animals to be found in ORIGAMI SAFARI, try folding a baby penguin from a small square of paper.

COBRA

Habitat
Africa, southern Asia, the Malay Archipelago and the Philippines.

The folding of this particular model is based around the reverse fold. Even though it may appear difficult at first, the cobra can be folded quite easily.

You will need:
Square of paper, coloured on one side and white on the other

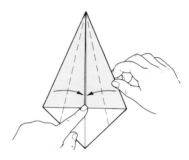

1 Repeat steps 1 and 2 of the PENGUIN on page 4. From the top point, fold the kite base's sloping sides in to meet the middle fold-line.

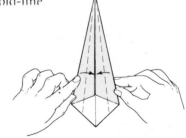

2 Again, from the top point, fold the sloping sides in to meet the middle fold-line.

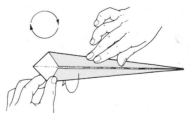

3 Turn the paper around into the position shown. Fold the bottom behind to the top.

5

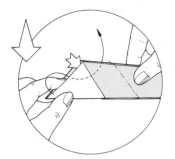

4 Now inside reverse fold the left-hand point. This is what you do, ...

8 Now outside reverse fold the head. This is what you do, separate the head's layers of paper, ...

11 Inside reverse fold the right-hand point down as shown.

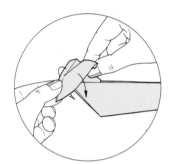

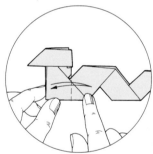

5 push the left-hand point up inside the model as shown.

9 taking one to the front and one to the back as shown. Press the paper flat, so making the cobra's hood.

12 Repeat steps 10 and 11 a few more times, so making the cobra's body.

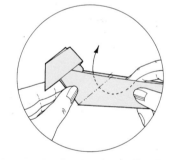

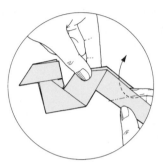

6 Press the paper flat, so making the cobra's head.

10 Inside reverse fold the right-hand point up as shown.

13 Fold the head and hood over at an angle. Press them flat and unfold them.

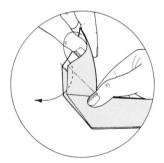

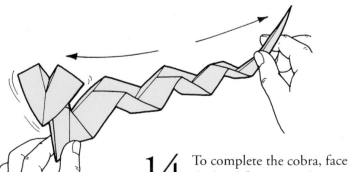

7 Inside reverse fold the cobra's head as shown.

14 To complete the cobra, face the head forward and open out its hood and body slightly.

SAVANNA GRASS/ BAMBOO LEAVES

Habitat

Savanna grass - found in open flat land in warm and sometimes wet part of the world. Bamboo - a tall plant of the grass family found especially in tropical areas.

Try folding some different sized savanna grasses and bamboo leaves to add that special something to your animal scenes.

You will need:

3 squares of paper all the same size, green on one side and white on the other

Glue

Narrow rectangle of green craft card

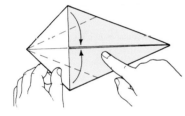

1 GRASS: Repeat steps 1 and 2 of the PENGUIN on page 4 with one square. Turn the kite base around into the position shown. From the left-hand point, fold the short sloping sides in to meet the middle fold-line, so making a shape that in origami is called the diamond base.

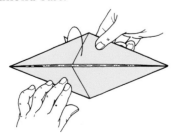

2 Fold the top behind to the bottom.

3 Inside reverse fold the right-hand point as shown.

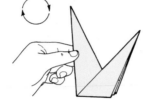

4 This should be the result.

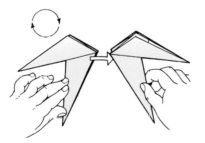

5 To complete the savanna grass, turn it around into the position shown.

6 BAMBOO LEAVES: Repeat steps 1 to 4 with the remaining two squares. Tuck the savanna grasses inside each other as shown. Glue them together.

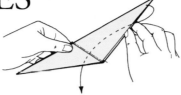

7 To complete the bamboo leaves, glue them on to the narrow rectangle of craft card as shown.

SEAL

Habitat

on or near coasts of all oceans of the world.

You can have a lot of fun folding this model, as well as learning how to fold a very important origami base.

You will need:

2 squares of paper the same size, black or brown, or grey on one side and white on the other
Scissors

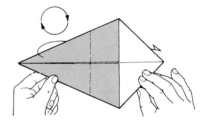

1 FEMALE: Repeat steps 1 and 2 of the PENGUIN on page 4 with one square of paper. Turn the kite base around into the position shown. Fold the left-hand point behind to the right-hand point.

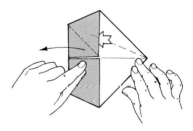

2 Pull the top flap of paper over ...

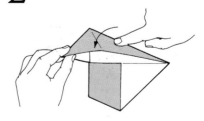

3 to the left, so its sloping edge meets the middle-fold line. Press the paper flat, to

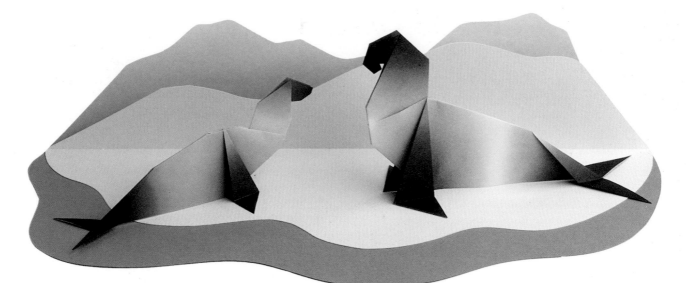

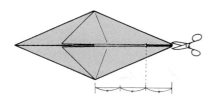

4 make a triangular pointed flap. Repeat steps 2 to 4 with the bottom flap of paper, so making a shape that in origami is called the fish base.

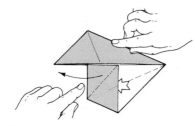

5 Fold the bottom right-hand point to the left as shown.

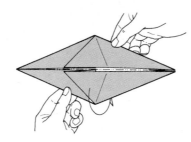

6 From the right-hand point, cut along the middle fold-line as far as shown, so making the seal's back flippers.

7 Fold the bottom behind to the top.

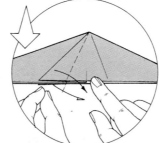

8 Fold the triangular flap over as shown, so making a front flipper. Repeat behind.

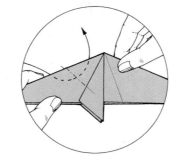

9 Inside reverse fold the left-hand point as shown.

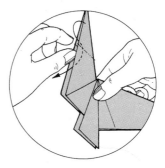

10 Again, reverse fold the left-hand point as shown, so making the seal's head.

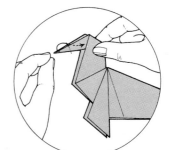

11 Blunt the head with an inside reverse fold.

12 Fold the front flipper up. Repeat behind.

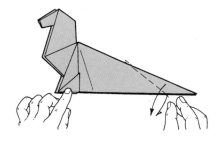

13 Fold the back flipper down. Repeat behind.

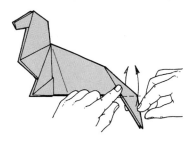

14 Fold the back flipper up. Repeat behind.

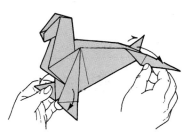

15 To complete the female seal, fold down its front flippers slightly and spread the back ones apart.

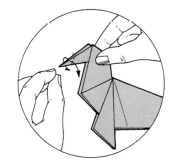

16 MALE: Repeat steps 1 to 10 with the remaining square. Outside reverse fold the head's tip, so making a snout. To complete, repeat steps 12 to 15.

OSTRICH

Habitat
the Sahara Desert and the dry table-lands of south-eastern Africa.

It is possible to make a sitting ostrich if you don't make the ostrich's legs.

You will need:
3 squares of paper all the same size, one square black on both sides for the ostrich's body and two squares white on both sides for its head and legs

Glue

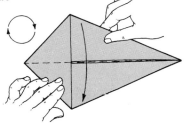

1 BODY: Repeat steps 1 and 2 of the PENGUIN on page 4 with the black square. Turn the kite base around into the position shown. Fold the top down to the bottom.

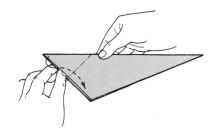

2 Inside reverse fold the left-hand point as shown.

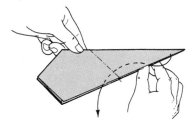

3 Inside reverse fold the right-hand point downwards.

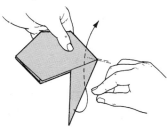

4 Inside reverse fold the right-hand point upwards.

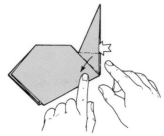

5 Insert a finger between the right-hand point's layers of paper as shown. Open them out and …

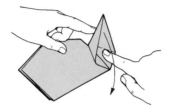

6 with your free hand, press the paper down into …

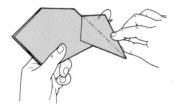

7 a diamond shape. Fold the diamond's upper sloping edges behind as shown, so …

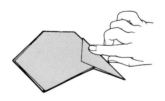

8 completing the body.

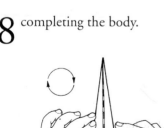

9 HEAD: Repeat steps 1 and 2 of the COBRA on page 5 with one white square. Turn the paper around into the position shown. Fold it in half from right to left.

10 Inside reverse fold the top point, so making the ostrich's head.

11 Double reverse fold the head as shown, so …

12 making the beak. To complete the head, press it flat.

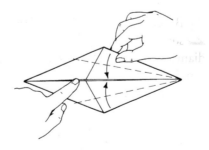

13 LEGS: Repeat step 1 of the SAVANNA GRASS on page 7 with the remaining white square. From the right-hand point, fold the sloping sides in to meet the middle fold-line.

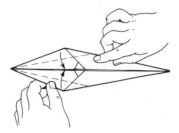

14 From the left-hand point, fold the sloping sides in to meet the middle fold-line.

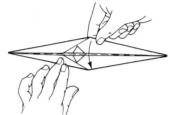

15 Fold the top down to the bottom.

16 Fold in half from right to left.

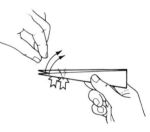

17 Double reverse fold both left-hand points as shown, so making the ostrich's feet. To complete the legs, press them flat.

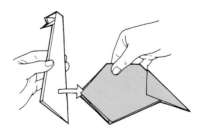

18 OSTRICH ASSEMBLY: Insert the ostrich's head into the body as shown.

19 Treating the inside left-hand points as if they were one, fold them ...

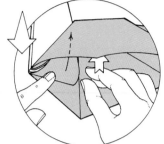

20 up inside the body, so locking the head and body together.

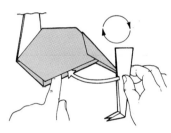

21 Insert the ostrich's legs into the body as shown. Glue them together.

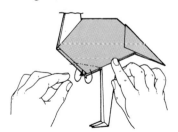

22 Fold the lower left-hand point up inside the body. Repeat behind.

23 Here is the completed ostrich.

MONKEY

Habitat

forests in Africa, Asia, Mexico through Central and South America.

Nearly all of the animals to be found in ORIGAMI SAFARI are based around the following body units.

You will need:

4 squares of paper all the same size, brown on one side and white on the other

Scissors

Glue

TAIL

1 TAIL: From one square, cut out a rectangle for the tail to the size shown.

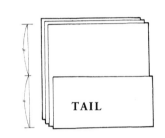

2 BODY UNIT A: Turn one square around to look like a diamond, with the white side on top. Fold it in half from right to left, so making a triangle.

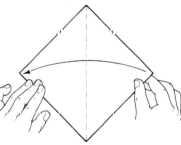

3 Fold the triangle in half from top to bottom.

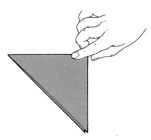

4 To complete body unit A, press it flat.

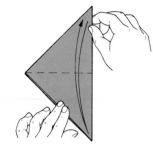

5 BODY UNIT B: Repeat step 2 with another square. Fold and unfold the triangle in half from top to bottom.

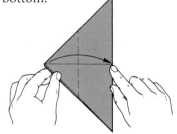

6 Fold the left-hand points over to meet the middle of the right-hand side.

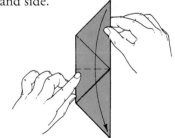

7 Fold in half from top to bottom.

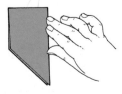

8 To complete body unit B, press it flat.

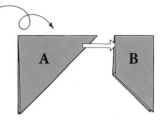

9 Turn body unit A over from side to side. Insert it into body unit B as shown. Glue them together.

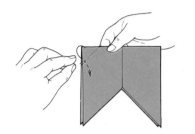

10 To complete the body, inside reverse fold a little of its top left-hand corner.

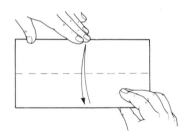

11 TAIL: Place the tail's rectangle sideways on, with the white side on top. Fold and unfold it in half from bottom to top.

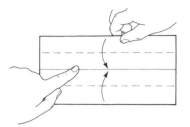

12 Fold the top and bottom edges in to meet the middle fold-line, so making a shape that in origami is called the cupboard fold.

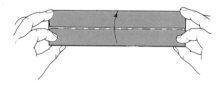

13 Fold in half from bottom to top.

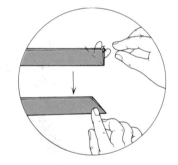

14 Fold the top right-hand corner down inside the cupboard fold. Repeat behind.

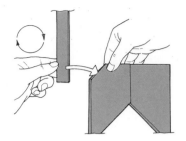

15 Turn tail around and insert it into the body as shown. Glue them together. Outside reverse fold the tail, so …

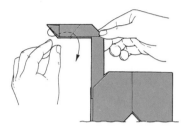

16 that it points towards the left. To complete the tail, inside reverse fold it downwards.

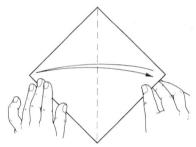

17 HEAD: Turn the remaining square around to look like a diamond, with the white side on top. Fold and unfold it in half from side to side.

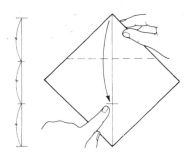

18 Fold the top point down as far as shown.

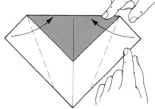

19 Fold the right- and left-hand short sloping sides over to lie along the top edge.

20 Fold the bottom point behind as far as shown.

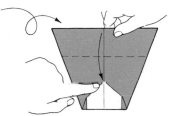

21 Turn the paper over from side to side. Fold the top edge down to meet the bottom point.

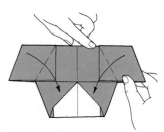

22 Fold the right- and left-hand short sloping edges over as shown.

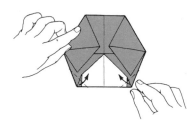

23 Fold over a little of each bottom point.

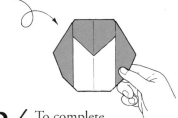

24 To complete the head, turn it over from side to side.

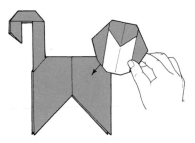

25 To complete the monkey, glue the head on to the body at the desired angle.

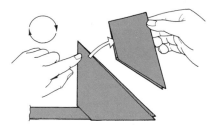

26 To make a sitting monkey, repeat steps 1 to 24, but in step 9 turn body unit A around and insert it into body unit B at an angle as shown. And, in steps 15 and 16, reverse fold the tail to fit your requirements.

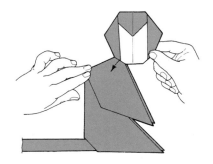

27 To complete, repeat step 25.

ZEBRA

Habitat
savanna and open forests of eastern Africa.

Do try to fold this origami model accurately otherwise your finished zebra will not look neat and tidy.

You will need:
4 squares of paper all the same size, white on both sides

Scissors

Glue

Black felt-tip pen

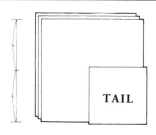

1 TAIL: From one square, cut out a square for the tail to the size shown.

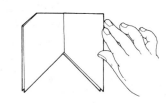

2 BODY: Repeat steps 2 to 10 of the MONKEY on page 11 with two squares.

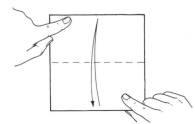

3 TAIL: Fold and unfold the tail's square in half from bottom to top.

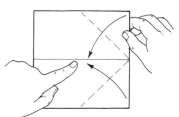

4 Fold the top and bottom right-hand corners in to meet the middle fold-line.

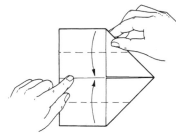

5 Fold the top and bottom edges in to meet the middle fold-line.

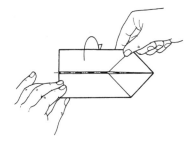

6 Fold the top half behind to the bottom.

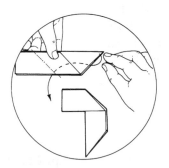

7 Inside reverse fold the right-hand point downwards as shown.

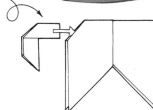

8 To complete the tail, turn it over from side to side. Insert the tail into the body as shown. Glue them together.

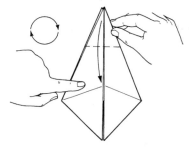

9 HEAD: Repeat steps 1 to 4 of the SEAL on page 7 with the remaining square. Turn the fish base around into the position shown. Fold its top point down ...

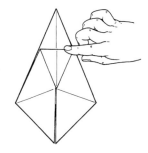

10 as far as shown, so making the zebra's ears.

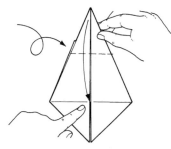

11 Turn the paper over from side to side. Fold the top point down as far as shown.

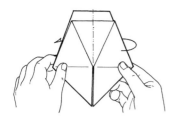

12 Fold the right-hand side behind to the left-hand side.

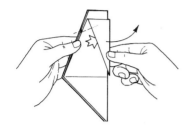

13 Holding the paper as shown, pull the point upwards, so it becomes free and sticks out from the folded side.

14 Blunt the point and shape the ears with inside reverse folds as shown.

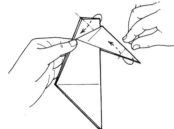

15 Here is the completed head.

16 Glue the head onto the body as shown. To complete the zebra, draw on its stripes with the black felt-tip pen.

TIGER

Habitat

variable, including most forest types of Asia, from India to Siberia and Java.

When making this model try hard to find the right colour of paper as this will make it look more realistic.

You will need:

4 squares of paper all the same size, orange on one side and white on the other

Scissors

Glue

Black felt-tip pen

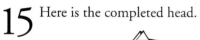

1 HEAD AND TAIL: From one square, cut the head's square and from another, cut out the tail's rectangle to the sizes shown.

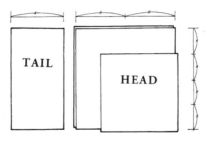

2 BODY UNIT A: Repeat steps 2 to 4 of the MONKEY on page 11 with one square.

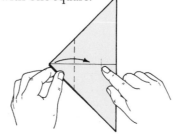

3 BODY UNIT B: Repeat step 5 of the MONKEY on page 11 with the remaining square. Fold the left-hand points over as far as shown.

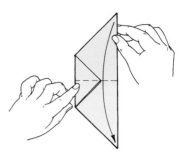

4 To complete body unit B, fold it in half from top to bottom.

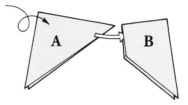

5 Turn body unit A over from side to side. Insert it into body unit B at a sloping angle as shown. Glue them together.

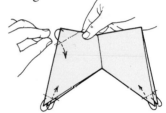

6 To complete the tiger's body, inside reverse fold a little of its top left-hand corner and bottom points as shown.

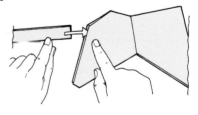

7 TAIL: Repeat steps 11 to 14 of the MONKEY on page 12 with the tail's rectangle. Insert the tail into the body as shown. Glue them together.

8 To complete the tail, inside reverse fold it upwards.

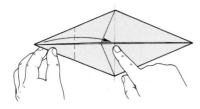

9 HEAD: Repeat step 1 of the SAVANNA GRASS on page 7 with the head's square. Fold the left-hand point in to the diamond base's middle.

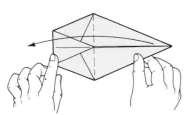

10 Fold the right-hand point over to the left on a line between the top and bottom points.

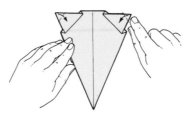

11 Turn the paper around into the position shown. Fold the top points down and then back up, so making small pleats.

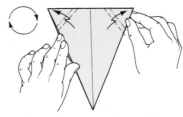

12 Fold over a little of each top point.

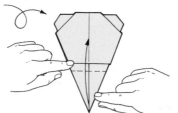

13 Turn the paper over from side to side. Fold the bottom point up as far as shown.

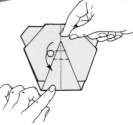

14 Fold the point over, and over again.

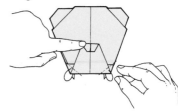

15 To complete the head, fold behind a little of each bottom point.

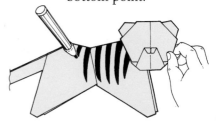

16 Glue the head on to the body at the desired angle. To complete the tiger, draw on its stripes with the black felt-tip pen.

LION FAMILY

Habitat

the African savanna and scrub; in India, Asia, it has adapted to forest life.

As each member of the lion family is made up of similar units, be very careful not to get the folding steps mixed up.

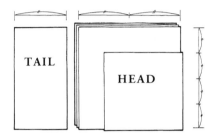

1 MALE: Fold and unfold one square in half from side to side. Cut along the middle fold-line, so making two rectangles. Put one rectangle to one side as it will be required for the female's tail. From another square, cut out a square for the head to the size shown.

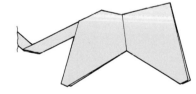

2 BODY AND TAIL: Repeat steps 2 to 8 of the TIGER on page 15 with two squares and the tail's rectangle.

You will need:

MALE - 5 squares of paper all the same size, brownish yellow on one side and white on the other
FEMALE - 3 squares of paper the same size and colour as the male's squares
CUB - 4 squares of paper that are half the size of and the same colour as the male's squares
Scissors
Glue

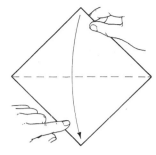

3 HEAD: Repeat steps 9 to 15 of the TIGER on page 16 with the head's square.

4 MANE: Turn the remaining square around to look like a diamond, with the white side on top. Fold it in half from top to bottom, so making an upside-down triangle.

5 Fold and unfold the triangle in half from side to side.

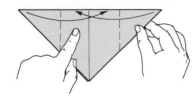

6 Fold the top points over, so that they overlap.

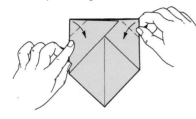

7 Fold over a little of each top point.

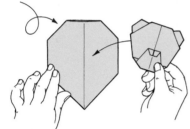

8 To complete the mane, turn it over from side to side. Glue the male's head on to the mane as shown.

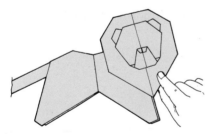

9 To complete the male, glue the mane onto the body at the desired angle.

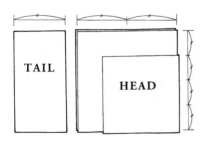

10 FEMALE: Cut out a square for the head to the size shown.

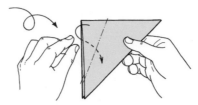

11 BODY UNIT A: Repeat steps 2 to 4 of the MONKEY on page 11 with one square. Turn body unit A over from side to side. To complete unit A, inside reverse fold its top left-hand point as shown.

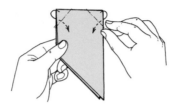

12 Body unit B: Repeat steps 5 to 8 of the MONKEY on page 11 with the remaining square. To complete body unit B, inside reverse fold a little of each top point as shown.

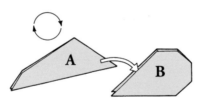

13 Turn body unit A around. Insert it into body unit B as shown. Glue them together.

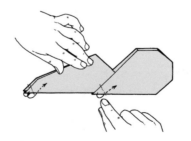

14 To complete the body, inside reverse fold the points as shown. Repeat behind.

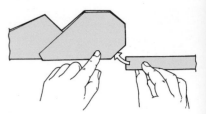

15 TAIL: Repeat steps 11 to 14 of the MONKEY on page 12 with the tail's rectangle (see step 1). Insert the tail into the body as shown. Glue them together.

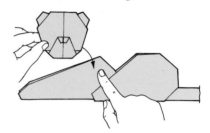

16 HEAD: Repeat steps 9 to 15 of the TIGER on page 16 with the head's square. To complete the female, glue the head onto the body at the desired angle.

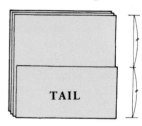

17 CUB: From one square, cut out the rectangle for the tail to the size shown.

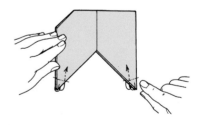

18 BODY: Repeat steps 2 to 10 of the MONKEY on page 11 with two squares. To complete the body, inside reverse fold the bottom points as shown. Repeat behind.

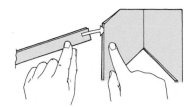

19 TAIL: Repeat steps 11 to 14 of the MONKEY page 12 with the tail's rectangle (see step 17). Insert the tail into the body as shown. Glue them together.

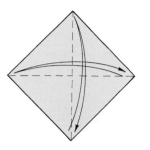

20 HEAD: Fold the remaining square's opposite corners and points together in turn to mark the diagonal fold-lines, with the coloured side on top, then open up again.

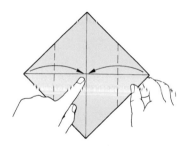

21 Fold the right- and left-hand corners in to meet the middle.

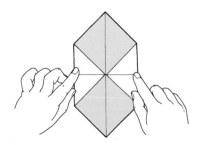

22 This should be the result.

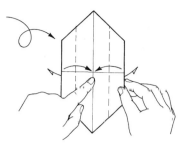

23 Turn the paper over from side to side. Fold the sides in to meet the middle, while at the same time letting the corners from underneath flick up.

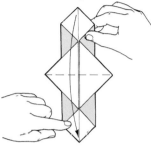

24 Fold the paper in half from top to bottom.

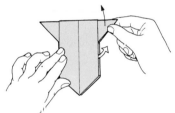

25 Pull the right-hand point up ...

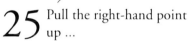

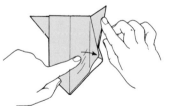

26 as far as shown, so making an ear. Press the paper flat.

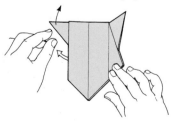

27 Repeat steps 25 and 26 with the left-hand point.

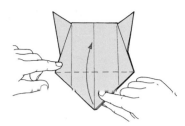

28 Fold the bottom points up.

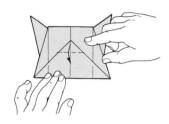

29 Fold the bottom points back down, so making a small upside down triangle.

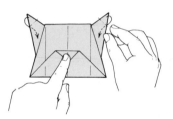

30 Inside reverse fold the ears as shown

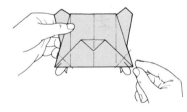

31 To complete the head, fold the lower right- and left-hand side points behind.

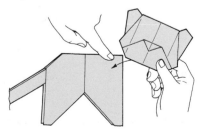

32 To complete the cub, glue the head onto the body at the desired angle.

HIPPOPOTAMUS

Habitat
rivers and lakes, surrounded by grassland, of Sub-Saharan Africa.

This model is very easy to fold. Do not be discouraged by the tricky folds in steps 4 to 7; they all fall into place very easily.

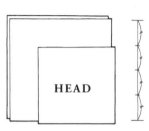

1 HEAD: From one square, cut out a square for the head to the size shown.

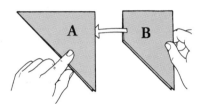

2 BODY UNITS A AND B: Repeat steps 2 to 4 of the TIGER on page 15 with the remaining two squares. Insert body unit B into body unit A as shown. Glue them together.

You will need:
3 squares of paper all the same size, grey on one side and white on the other

Scissors

Glue

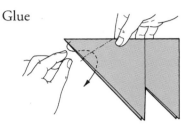

3 Inside reverse fold the left-hand point.

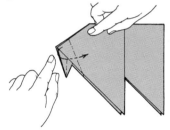

4 Narrow down the reversed point. This is what you do, …

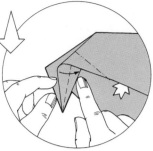

5 fold the top layer of the point in half, at the same time pushing the triangular area inwards as shown by the line of dots and dashes.

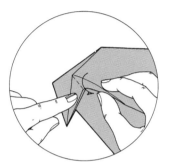

6 This shows step 5 taking place.

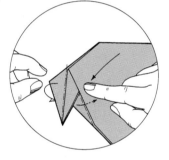

7 Repeat steps 4 to 6 behind, so making the hippopotamus's tail.

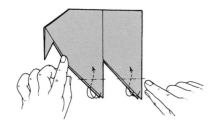

8 To complete the body, inside reverse fold the bottom points as shown.

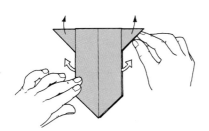

9 HEAD: Repeat steps 20 to 24 of the LION CUB on page 19 with the head's square . Pull each top point up ...

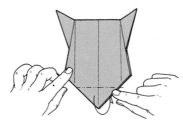

10 as far away as shown so making the ears. Fold the bottom points behind.

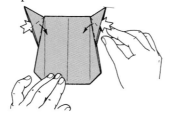

11 Open out each ear and press it down neatly into a diamond shape.

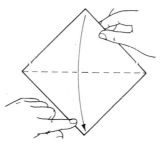

12 Open out each ear, so that it ...

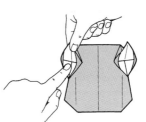

13 becomes three-dimensional as shown.

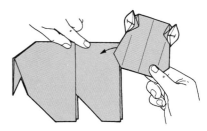

14 To complete the hippopotamus, glue the head on to the body at the desired angle.

ELEPHANT

Habitat

semidesert, forest to plains of Africa, India, the Indochinese peninsula, Sumatra and Sri Lanka.

With just a few folds you can make a marvellous elephant.

You will need:

3 squares of paper all the same size, grey on one side and white on the other

Glue

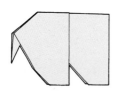

1 BODY: Repeat steps 2 to 8 of the HIPPOPOTAMUS on page 20 with two squares.

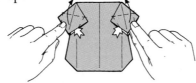

2 HEAD: Turn the remaining square around to look like a diamond, with the white side on top. Fold it in half from top to bottom, so making an upside down triangle.

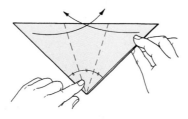

3 Fold the right-hand side over to a point one-third of the way across the triangle. Repeat with the left-hand side so that it lies on top.

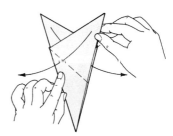

4 Fold the top points over to either side, so making the ears.

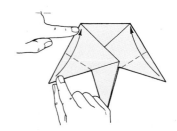

5 Fold the ears in half as shown.

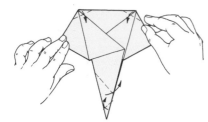

6 Fold over a little of each top point. Make the elephant's trunk by folding the bottom point as shown.

7 This should be the result. To complete the head, turn it over from side to side.

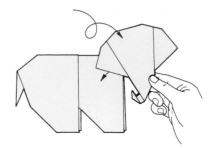

8 To complete the elephant, glue the head on to the body at the desired angle. For a more realistic looking elephant, cut out a set of tusks from a piece of thin white card and glue them either side of the trunk, as shown in the photograph below.

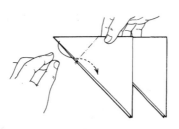
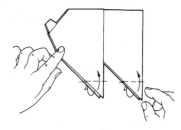

POLAR BEAR

Habitat
the snow and ice fields of the Northern Polar regions.

By using different shades of paper it is possible to make many different species of bears.

You will need:
3 squares of paper all the same size, white on both sides

Glue

1 BODY: Repeat step 2 of the HIPPOPOTAMUS on page 20 with two squares. Inside reverse fold the left-hand point.

2 Reverse fold the point back out, so making the polar bear's tail.

3 Blunt the tail with an inside reverse fold. Fold the left-hand side point inside the body. Repeat behind.

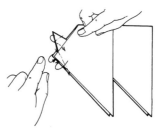

4 Fold the bottom points up. Repeat behind.

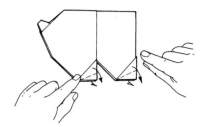

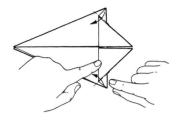

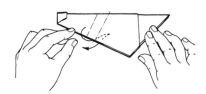

5 Fold the bottom points down as shown, so making the paws. Repeat behind.

8 Fold the top and bottom points over the pleats.

11 Double reverse fold the nose as shown (see steps 9 to 11 of the PENGUIN on page 5).

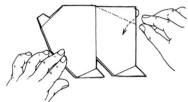

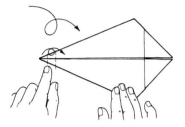

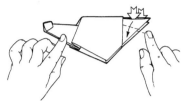

6 To complete the body, inside reverse fold the top right-hand point as shown.

9 Turn the paper over from top to bottom. Treating the left-hand side points as if they were one, fold them over and over again, so making the bear's nose.

12 To complete the head, open out the right-hand points slightly, so making the ears.

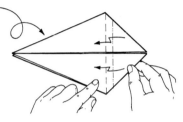

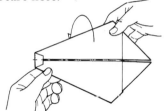

7 HEAD: Repeat steps 1 to 4 of the SEAL on page 7 with the remaining square. Turn the fish base over from side to side. Fold the top and bottom triangular points to the left and back to the right, so making small pleats.

10 Fold the top behind to the bottom.

13 Turn the head over. To complete the polar bear, glue the head onto the body at the desired angle.

WHITE RHINOCEROS

Habitat

the grasslands, savanna; also near swamps and rivers of southern Sudan and South Africa.

The white rhinoceros is actually light grey in colour, so try to use the correct coloured paper.

You will need:

3 squares of paper all the same size, light grey on one side and white on the other

Glue

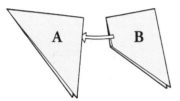

1 BODY UNITS A AND B: Repeat steps 2 to 4 of the TIGER on page 15 with two squares. Insert body unit B into body unit A at a sloping angle as shown. Glue them together.

2 Repeat steps 3 to 7 of the HIPPOPOTAMUS on page 20, so making the tail.

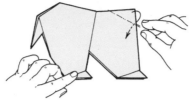

3 Repeat steps 4 and 5 of the POLAR BEAR on page 22, so making the feet. To complete the body, inside reverse fold the top right-hand point as shown.

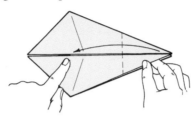

4 HEAD: Repeat steps 1 to 5 of the SEAL on page 7 with the remaining square. Fold the top right-hand point over as far as shown, so making the back horn.

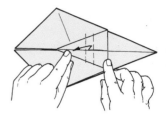

5 Fold the back horn to the right and back to the left, so making a small pleat.

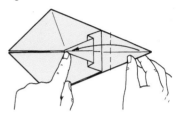

6 Fold the bottom right-hand point over as far as shown, so making the front horn.

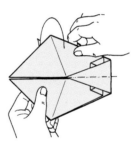

7 Fold the top behind to the bottom.

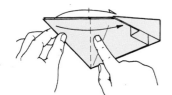

8 Fold the left-hand triangular flap over to the right. Repeat behind.

9 Fold the triangular flap over to meet the left-hand side, so making an ear. Repeat behind.

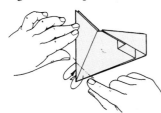

10 Fold the lower left-hand point up inside the head. Repeat behind.

11 Pull the front horn up, pressing it flat into the position shown in step 12.

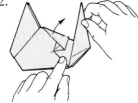

12 To complete the head, pull the back horn up, pressing it flat into the position shown in step 13.

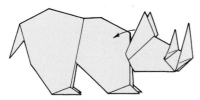

13 To complete the white rhinoceros, glue the head on to the body at the desired angle.

GIRAFFE

Habitat

the savanna, sparse scrub of sub-Saharan Africa.

By making slight variations in the folds, you can easily create a running or feeding giraffe.

You will need:

3 squares of paper all the same size, yellow on one side and white on the other

Glue

Brown felt-tip pen

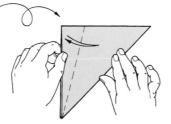

1 BODY: Repeat steps 2 to 4 of the MONKEY on page 11 with one square. Turn the unit over from side to side. Fold and unfold the unit's left-hand side, as shown.

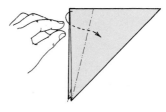

2 Using the fold-lines made in step 1 as a guide, inside reverse fold the unit's left-hand side. Repeat steps 1 and 2 with another square.

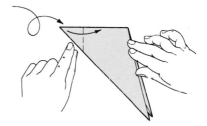

3 Turn one unit over from side to side. Fold the top left-hand point over towards the right.

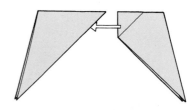

4 Insert one unit inside the other as shown. Glue them together.

5 To complete the body, inside reverse fold the right-hand point, so making the tail.

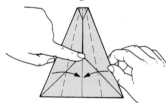

6 HEAD: Repeat steps 1 and 2 of the PENGUIN on page 4 with the remaining square. Fold over a little of the top point. Fold the white triangle up along the base of the coloured triangle.

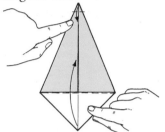

7 From the top edge, fold the sloping sides in to meet the middle fold-line.

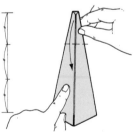

8 Fold the top edge over as far as shown, so making the head.

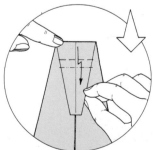

9 Fold the head up and then back down, so making a small pleat.

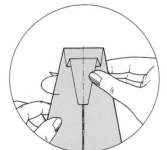

10 Fold the left-hand side behind to the right-hand side.

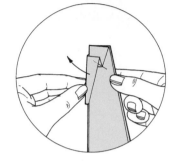

11 Pull up the head as far as the pleat will allow you.

12 Pull out the head's inside layer of paper. Repeat behind.

13 To complete the head, inside reverse fold the top left-hand point, so making the ears.

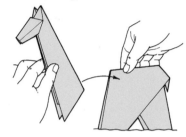

14 Glue the head onto the body at the desired angle.

15 To complete the giraffe, draw on its spots with the brown felt-tip pen.

GAZELLE

Habitat
desert, to the edge of the Sahel - Saharan Africa.

Remember to fold neatly and look very carefully at each illustration to see what you should do.

You will need:
3 squares of paper all the same size, reddish brown on one side and white on the other

Glue

Scissors

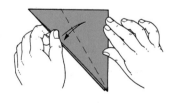

1 BODY: Repeat steps 2 to 4 of the MONKEY on page 11 with one square. Fold and unfold the unit's left-hand sloping side as shown.

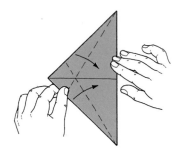

2 Unfold the unit from bottom to top to make a triangle. Using the fold-lines made in step 1 as a guide, fold over the triangle's sloping sides.

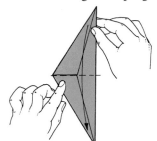

3 Fold the triangle in half from top to bottom, so making the gazelle's back legs.

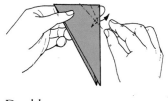

4 Double reverse fold the top right-hand corner of the legs as shown, so making the tail.

5 Repeat step 5 of the MONKEY on page 11 with another square. Fold and unfold the triangle in half from left to right.

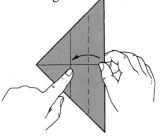

6 Fold the triangle's right-hand side over to meet the fold-line made in step 5.

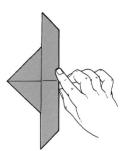

7 This should be the result.

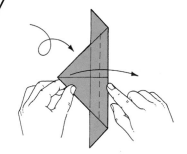

8 Turn the paper over from top to bottom. Fold the left-hand point over, so that the fold-line made in step 5 lies along the right-hand side.

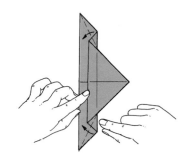

9 Fold the top and bottom right-hand points over as shown.

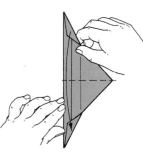

10 Fold in half from top to bottom, so making the front legs.

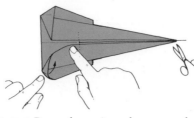

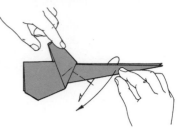

11 Insert the front legs into the back legs as shown. Glue them together.

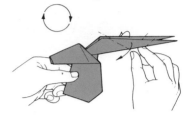

12 Here is the completed body.

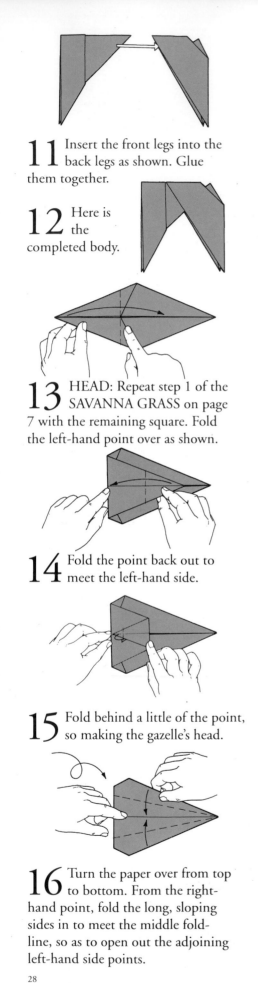

13 HEAD: Repeat step 1 of the SAVANNA GRASS on page 7 with the remaining square. Fold the left-hand point over as shown.

14 Fold the point back out to meet the left-hand side.

15 Fold behind a little of the point, so making the gazelle's head.

16 Turn the paper over from top to bottom. From the right-hand point, fold the long, sloping sides in to meet the middle fold-line, so as to open out the adjoining left-hand side points.

17 Press the points down neatly into triangles. From the right-hand point, cut along the middle fold-line as far as shown, so making the gazelle's horns.

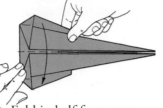

18 Fold in half from top to bottom.

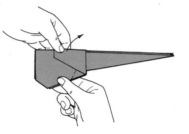

19 Pull up the head and press it flat, into the position shown in step 20.

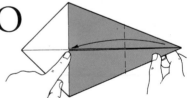

20 Fold the front horn over as shown. Repeat behind.

21 Turn the head around into the position shown. To complete the head, shape the horns by folding them down and then back up.

22 To complete the gazelle, glue the head on to the body at the desired angle.

RED KANGAROO

Habitat
the arid grassland, scrub and salt plains throughout inland continental Australia.

As with all origami animals, try changing the angle of the folds especially those of the tail, legs and ears, to see how many new animals you can create.

You will need:
3 squares of paper all the same size, reddish brown on one side and white on the other

Glue

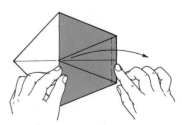

1 BODY: Repeat steps 1 and 2 of the PENGUIN on page 4 with one square. Turn the kite base around into the position shown. Fold the right-hand point over as shown.

2 Fold the point back out towards the right, so making a small pleat.

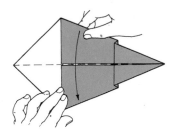

3 Fold in half from top to bottom.

4 Pull up the point as far as the hidden pleat will allow you, so making the kangaroo's tail.

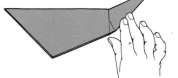

5 To complete the body, press the paper flat.

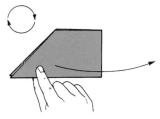

6 BACK LEGS: Repeat steps 5 to 8 of the MONKEY on page 11 with another square. Turn body unit B around into the position shown. Open it out from left to right.

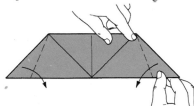

7 Fold the right- and left-hand side points over, into the position shown in step 8.

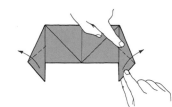

8 Fold the points back up, into the position shown in step 9.

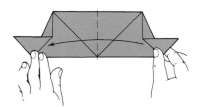

9 To complete the back legs, fold them in half from right to left.

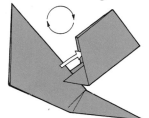

10 Insert the body into the back legs as shown. Glue them together.

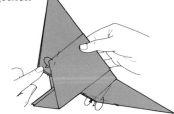

11 To complete the body, shape the tail by folding its bottom points up inside and the legs by folding their top points behind as shown.

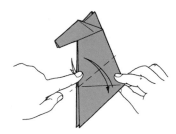

12 HEAD AND FRONT PAWS: Repeat steps 9 to 15 of the ZEBRA on page 14 with the remaining square. Fold the triangular pointed flaps towards the left. Press them flat and unfold them.

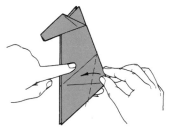

13 Fold the right-hand side point over as shown. Repeat behind.

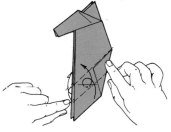

14 To complete the head, fold the triangular pointed flaps over, and over again so making the front paws.

15 To complete the Kangaroo, glue the head and front paws onto the body at the desired angle.

KOALA

Habitat

the eucalypt forest and woodlands of eastern and southwestern coastal Australia.

This Koala is a perfect example of an origami technique that uses just a few major folds to create the animal's main features.

You will need:

2 squares of paper the same size, grey on both sides

Scissors

Glue

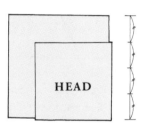

1 HEAD: From one square, cut out a square for the head to the size shown.

2 BODY: Fold and unfold the remaining square in half from bottom to top and side to side.

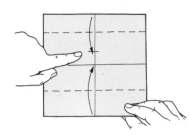

3 Fold the bottom edge in to meet the middle fold-line. Fold the top edge down as far as shown.

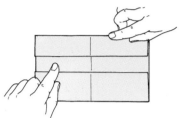

4 This should be the result.

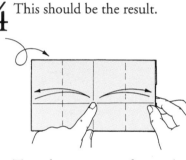

5 Turn the paper over from side to side. Fold the sides in to meet the middle fold-line. Press them flat and unfold them.

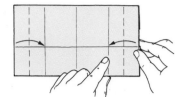

6 Fold the sides in to meet the fold-lines made in step 5.

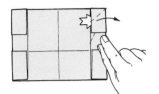

7 Insert your forefinger underneath the top right-hand layer of paper as shown, and …

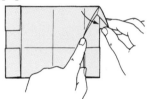

8 open out the top layer.

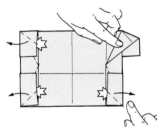

9 Press the paper down neatly into the position shown. Repeat steps 7 to 9 with the bottom right-hand layer and the top and bottom left-hand layers.

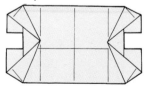

10 This should be the result.

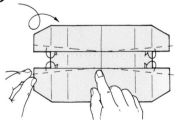

11 Turn the paper over from side to side. Fold each middle point behind as shown.

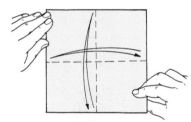

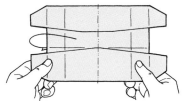

12 Fold the left-hand side behind to the right-hand side.

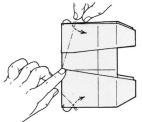

13 To complete the body, inside reverse fold the top and bottom left-hand points as shown.

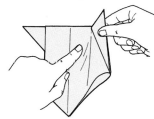

14 HEAD: Repeat steps 20 to 24 of the LION CUB on page 19 with the head's square. Pull each top point up as far as shown, so making the ears.

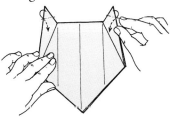

15 Inside reverse fold the tip of each ear.

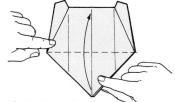

16 Fold the bottom points up as shown, so making a triangle.

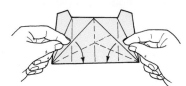

17 Fold the triangle's sloping sides down to meet the bottom edge, while at the same time …

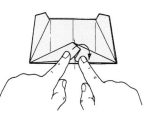

18 flattening the triangle to the right with its sides still folded together, so making a triangular flap.

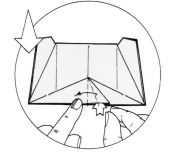

19 Open out the triangular flap and press it down neatly into a diamond.

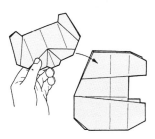

20 Fold behind a little of the diamond's tip. To complete the head, fold the right- and left-hand bottom points behind.

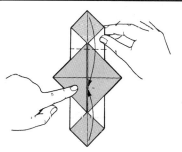

21 To complete the koala, glue the head onto the body at the desired angle.

GIANT PANDA

Habitat
the bamboo forests of South central China.

This model is very easy to fold and it will bring you plenty of oohs and ahs from your friends!

You will need:
2 squares of paper the same size, black on one side and white on the other

Glue

1 BODY: Repeat steps 2 to 13 of the KOALA on page 30 with one square, but with the white side on top in step 2.

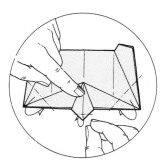

2 HEAD: Repeat steps 20 to 23 of the LION CUB on page 19 with the remaining square, but with the white side on top in step 20. Fold the top and bottom points over as far as shown.

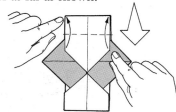

3 Fold the top point back up, so that its side points meet the top edge.

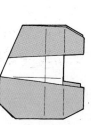

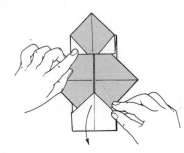

4 Unfold the bottom point.

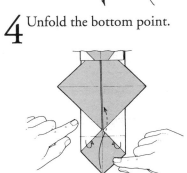

5 Using the fold-lines made in step 2 as a guide, reverse fold the bottom point up inside the model as shown.

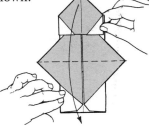

6 Fold the top point down on a line between the two side points.

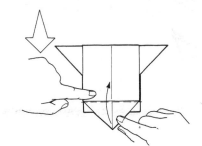

7 Fold the bottom point up, so making a coloured triangle.

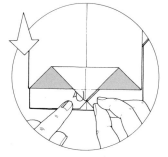

8 Fold the triangle's tip down as far as shown.

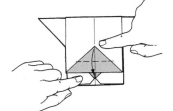

9 Fold the triangle's tip behind up inside the model.

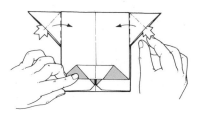

10 Open out each side point and press them down neatly into diamonds.

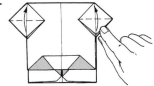

11 Fold one diamond's front flap up, so making an ear. Repeat with the other diamond.

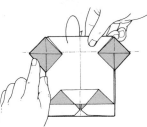

12 Fold the top edge behind on a line between the ears as shown.

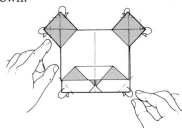

13 Shape the ears by folding their top and side points behind. To complete the head, fold the right- and left-hand bottom points behind.

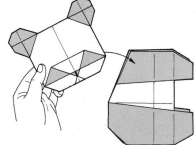

14 To complete the panda, glue the head on to the body at the desired angle.